For RJ

MYRIAD BOOKS LIMITED
35 Bishopsthorpe Road, London SE26 4PA

First published in 2004 by
PICCADILLY PRESS LIMITED
5 Castle Road, London NW1 8PR
www.piccadillypress.co.uk

ISBN 1 905606 19 2
EAN 9 781905 606 191

Designed by Fielding Design Ltd

Printed in China

Fairy Hill

The Summer Ball

Fran Evans

MYRIAD BOOKS LIMITED

The sun was slowly rising over Fairy Hill.
Bees were buzzing and birds were singing
sweetly.
Today was a special day. It was the day
of the Summer Ball, when all the fairies
in the kingdom dressed in costumes and
danced from dusk until dawn.

At this early hour of the morning, however, all the fairies were asleep – except for one . . .

Rose Fairy was a dressmaker. She was creating
beautiful costumes for all the fairies, and she had
not had a wink of sleep.

She collected petals, posies and precious trinkets
to decorate the wonderful dresses, caps and capes.
Costumes and decorations filled every nook and
cranny in her tiny house.

Rose Fairy hardly noticed the daylight. Glow flies flitted around, lighting up the room so that she could add the finishing touches.

"You must rest, Rose Fairy," they buzzed, "or you'll be too tired for the party."
"Just a few more stitches here . . . seeds on this one . . ." she muttered sleepily.

As the sun peeped in through their curtains, four fairies on Fairy Hill were too excited to sleep any longer. They jumped out of their beds and hurried to Rose Fairy's house.

Their costumes were ready and waiting, and the four friends could not believe their eyes.

"Oh, Rose Fairy, how hard you have worked! They're beautiful!" Ladybird Fairy exclaimed.

The costumes were a perfect fit and the fairies hopped, skipped and fluttered away in a flurry of excitement.

Not long after, there was a steady stream of
fairies arriving to collect their costumes.
There were blue beetle fairies . . .

slow snail fairies . . .

dancing dandelion fairies . . .

and bluebell fairies in their flower chariot.

At last, nearly all the costumes had been collected.
"Have you decided what *you* are going to wear, Rose
Fairy?" buzzed the glow flies.
"I have just one more dress to finish before I think of that,"
she replied wearily. Then she took out a special box from
under her bed.

Rose Fairy carefully selected some jewel-like seeds for
the magnificent dress. She hoped Queen Bee Fairy would
be pleased.

She was ever so tired, though, and as she stitched on the
final details, her eyelids began to feel heavy. She had to
rest, just for a moment . . .

Rat-a-tat-tat!

Queen Bee Fairy and Worker Bee Fairy had brought a large jar of wildflower honey to give to Rose Fairy.

But there was no answer at the door, so they stepped inside . . .

Rose Fairy didn't stir.

"Oh, poor Rose Fairy – she has exhausted herself finishing my beautiful costume!"
Worker Bee Fairy noticed a plain dress hanging by the door. "That must be Rose Fairy's costume for the ball," he whispered, "and she hasn't finished it! What are we to do?"

"I must find her friends," said Queen Bee Fairy
and she flew off into the forest.

After much searching, she found the four fairies practising their dancing in a ferny glade.

"Rose Fairy needs your help," Queen Bee Fairy said. "She is worn out from making our costumes and has nothing to wear to the ball."

The four friends arrived at Rose Fairy's house in no time
at all.
Ladybird Fairy examined the half-finished dress. "We have
to finish this," she said.
"But how?" asked Butterfly Fairy.

"This dress is so plain," said Grasshopper Fairy, panicking.
"We need to decorate it," said Dragonfly Fairy, "but there
is nothing left . . ."
Ladybird Fairy took charge.

"Dragonfly Fairy, you go down to the stream to collect some pretty pebbles . . .

"Grasshopper Fairy, go to the meadow and bring back some seeds and flowers . . ."

Through all of this, Rose Fairy did not wake.
The fairies snipped and sewed until the sun
had almost disappeared.

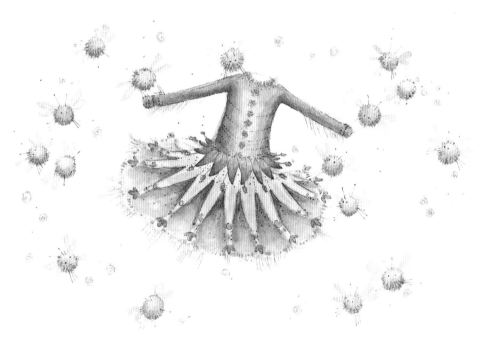

Then they selected tiny seeds, flowers and stones
to finish off the dress.

The fairies gently tried to wake their friend, but Rose Fairy was still sound asleep.
They carefully slipped the dress onto her and carried her to the ball on her rose petal carpet.

On the way, Rose Fairy opened her eyes, thinking she must
be in the middle of a beautiful dream . . .

But it was not a dream.

When they arrived at the ball, Rose Fairy looked around the room at all the costumes she had worked so hard to make.

Rose Fairy had never felt so special, for she knew that *her* costume had been made by her kindhearted friends.

It was a magical evening. All the fairies danced and sang and celebrated until the sun rose again over Fairy Hill.